Presto
Change-o

written and illustrated by
Audrey Wood

Child's Play (International) Ltd
Swindon   Auburn ME   Sydney
ion 2005
1 Croatia

Presto Change-O!
Zippity Zap!

Magic flowers, come out of my hat!

Matthew, just what do you think you're doing?
Rehearsing tricks for my magic show, Jessica.

Tricks? How boring! I can do real magic!

Presenting the fantastic
Queen of Magic! Watch and be amazed!

Go away, Jessica.
This is my show.

I'm the best magician.

You are not!

Oh, yes I am!

Children, please stop arguing. Your magic
will be better if you work together.

So there, Matthew! First,
I'll do Chinese Rings.

That's not *real* magic!

Real magic?

Gulp . . .

Hee, hee, I knew you
were just bragging.

Oh, yeah. . . See
this magic powder?

Presto Change-O,
Jiggledy Jog,

I'll turn a human. . .

. . . into a frog!

Where's Mother?

Look, there's a frog in her basket!

Jessica, I think you made a big mistake.

You changed Mother into a frog instead of me.

Well, don't just stand there. Change her back!

Presto Change-O, Frog to Mother!

Ugh!
Mother ate a fly!

It's all right, Mother.
That's what frogs do.

I'll try my magic.
Yours is nothing
but trouble.

Zippety Zap,
One-two-three,
Mother's back!

Catch her! She's escaping!

Mother!
Come down here
this minute!

Stop! You'll get lost in the rain!

Hurry!
She's jumping
into the woods!

Look! There she is!

SPLISH!   SPLASH!   SPLOT!

Now, we'll never find her.

She was such
a good Mother.

Even when
she was a frog.

This wouldn't have happened, if only
we had worked together like Mother said.

Together. . . that's it!

Zippity Zap,   Jiggledy Jog. . .

Now our Mother's not a frog!

Children! Where in the world
did you disappear to?
I've been looking everywhere!

Let's hurry!
Our magic has just begun!